WATTERS · LEYH · BRYANT · LAIHO

LUMBERJANES™

SMITTEN IN THE STARS

Published by
BOOM! BOX™

BOOM! BOX™

LUMBERJANES Volume Seventeen, February 2021. Published by BOOM! Box, a division of Boom Entertainment, Inc.

BOOM! Studios, 5670 Wilshire Boulevard, Suite 400, Los Angeles, CA 90036-5679. Printed in USA. First Printing.

ISBN: 978-1-68415-667-2, eISBN: 978-1-64668-152-5

THIS LUMBERJANES FIELD MANUAL BELONGS TO:

NAME: ______________________________

TROOP: ______________________________

DATE INVESTED: ______________________________

FIELD MANUAL TABLE OF CONTENTS

A Message from the Lumberjanes High Council........ **4**
The Lumberjanes Pledge........ **4**
Counselor Credits........ **5**

LUMBERJANES PROGRAM FIELDS
Chapter Sixty-Five........ **6**
Chapter Sixty-Six........ **30**
Chapter Sixty-Seven........ **54**
Chapter Sixty-Eight........ **78**
Cover Gallery: It's a Myth-Tery Badge........ **103**

LUMBERJANES FIELD MANUAL

For the Advanced Program

Tenth Edition • May 1985

Prepared for the

Miss Qiunzella Thiskwin Penniquiqul Thistle Crumpet's

CAMP FOR HARDCORE LADY-TYPES

"Friendship to the Max!"

A MESSAGE FROM THE LUMBERJANES HIGH COUNCIL

There is one high councilor who, as a child, came down with a case of summertime pneumonia. Many of us older Lumberjanes have similar stories, whether due to measles, chicken pox, or mumps—all illnesses which we sincerely hope will be the stuff of stories in years to come, just as scarlet fever and polio were for us, when we were children.

This high councilor, at the time just a little Sapling scout, had to stay cooped up in her hot, humid bedroom under piles of blankets. While all of her friends ran through sprinklers and played hopscotch and tag, she was wracked with fever, and too weak to partake in her favorite games. Songs on the radio made her cry, her friends waving to her through the windows or calling her up on the telephone made her ache to be hale and hearty and outside skipping rope with them. This stage of recovery is always an especially difficult one—a point at which you are not yet well, but you are also no longer so sick that you lack even the energy to wish that you were better.

But of course, eventually she did heal. Her lungs grew stronger. Her fever broke. She could speak without wheezing and walk without getting tired. Still, there was so much she had missed, and so much she would not get to do, with autumn right around the corner.

All this is to say: things will still be there for you, when you're able to come to them. Games are still played in autumn, and even in winter. Your friends will be excited to see you feeling well. The world will be waiting and ready, like spring primed to bloom after the frost. And while each new spring may not be the same as the one before it, it is always still spring. Even if you have been through hardships, and even if you find yourself a slightly different child than you were, and even if you need to come to this new spring in a different manner than you would have before...no matter what, it will still be spring. And you will still be you.

THE LUMBERJANES PLEDGE

I solemnly swear to do my best
Every day, and in all that I do,
To be brave and strong,
To be truthful and compassionate,
To be interesting and interested,
To pay attention and question
The world around me,
To think of others first,
To always help and protect my friends,
~~[illegible]~~
And to make the world a better place
For Lumberjane scouts
And for everyone else.

THEN THERE'S A LINE ABOUT GOD, OR WHATEVER

Written by
Shannon Watters & Kat Leyh

Illustrated by
Kanesha C. Bryant

Colors by
Maarta Laiho

Letters by
Aubrey Aiese

Cover by
Kat Leyh

Designer
Chelsea Roberts
Editor
Sophie Philips-Roberts
Executive Editor
Jeanine Schaefer

Special thanks to ***Kelsey Pate*** *for giving the Lumberjanes their name.*

Created by
Shannon Watters, Grace Ellis, Noelle Stevenson & Brooklyn Allen

LUMBERJANES FIELD MANUAL

CHAPTER SIXTY-FIVE

UGH.
How much FURTHER, Hes?

Hey, Barney, how about getting that cat of yours to carry all of us?!
Marigold prefers BEING the one carried most of the time, Diane!

What if you carried ME, then, huh? When's MY turn?
Haha! I can only carry one at a time!

Barney!

We FINALLY caught up to you!
Hi, April!

How much further is this "scenic outlook," anyway?

That's what I'M saying! Why can't we just watch this "whatever" back at camp?!

It's THE PERSEIDS, Diane!

Only the BEST meteor shower in this HEMISPHERE! We could be seeing up to 80 shooting stars an HOUR!
They're caused by COSMIC DEBRIS from meteors entering our atmosphere!
GASP! Will any land near us?!?!?!? Can we go... meteor hunting????

No, most pieces are actually super small. I think most burn up in the atmosphere.
Awww!
You know your stuff, Emily!

Thanks! Space is a hobby of mine. I actually wanted to talk with you about some of this...
Sure!
The Perseids are named after the constellation of the Greek hero Perseus, Diane! From mythology!
Yeah, yeah. I ALSO have meteors named after me. You people basically named all your coolest stuff after us Greek gods, who ELSE would you use?
PAT PAT

Molly was being NICE, Diane, and yet you've ALREADY made it about YOU.
I didn't make it about me! Scientists did, or whatever!

I don't remember any planets or stars called Diane!
Try Artemis, duh!

Like w--
Oop! Sorry!
BUMP!

BUMP!

S--
Watch it!
WOW. I was trying to apologize, JEEZ!

I think you're just jealous! What's named after YOU, huh?
A WHOLE MONTH!

PRETTY SURE THE MONTH CAME FIRST!
I have a MOON CRATER named after me, a bunch of stuff on Venus--
Yeah, but who's the PLANET named after?
GASP!

DON'T BRING MY SISTER INTO THIS!

?
Which planet is named after YOU, huh?!

Jo?

C'mon, you've had this fight...so... many...times
TRUE SAD

huff huff Thanks for coming!
huff What's going on, Emily?

So glad you asked, Jo, I th--
Hey!

Since when do we just run off into the woods without saying anything? **Anything** could be out here!

Exactly! As I was just explaining.
Excuse me...

...so we're just running off into the woods, now?
What are we? The Ro--
TRUE SAD

TRUE SAD

...The Roanokes?
Hey! We--

...I guess we DO do that a lot...
Why'd YOU run off after us, then?
You were acting weird.

I'm only out here looking after Emily! She's been actin' REAL squirrelly all day!
Yeah, what's up with you, Emily?

I am standing here, literally BUSTING to tell you guys what's up!!
So, let's hear it.

ALIENS! I'M HUNTING FOR SPACE ALIENS!
It's been my DREAM to find one since I was a kid! And I'm closer than EVER!
There have been some scattered sightings recently, but it's enough for me to have a good idea of where to look next!
And meteor showers are CLASSIC covers for alien activity! So, it has to be TODAY! NOW!

And I know Jo's into this kind of stuff, and so I thought she'd want to come along! To make *FIRST CONTACT!*
TRUE
I WOULD be into that...but...

ALIENS?! WOW!
I know, right?

APPEAR
THAT'S! SO! COOL!

Where did YOU come from?
TRUE SAD

That's just Ripley!
I get that a lot!

I WANNA COME! CAN I HELP?

"Honestly..."
TRUE SAD

...I don't like having to break up fights.
Sorry, Jen.
Sorry.

So, to keep you out of trouble...
OOF!

...you two are coming with me and helping me set the telescope up!

ATTENTION, SCOUTS!

WE HAVE ARRIVED!

EVERYONE FIND A GOOD SPOT AND SETTLE IN FOR THE SHOW!
AW YEAH!

Yeah! Woo-hoo!

MOLLY!

Sit with us!

Thanks, B. I don't know where my cabin disappeared to!
Half of ours is missing, too! We got separated in the rush.

Well, we know where SOME of our delinquents are...

Exercise the single shred of patience you have, Diane, and wait until it's SET. UP.

FINISH already! I'm gonna show you all my rad constellations!

I put up all the BEST ones...
I have a hard time believing you actually MADE any constellations...

Oh, yeah?
Girls...please... we are here to peacefully watch--

Watch THIS!

Uh...Diane...don't actually... MOVE anything, please?

The solar system is complic--
A SHOOTING STAR! I SAW ONE!

WHAT?! The SUN'S still up!
Didn't I?
You--you didn't do that!

Jen?
The stars aren't OUT yet!

Diane, STOP!
Admit I'm awesome!

I'm gonna make a constellation that looks like a BUTT and name it APRIL!
NOOOOO!
What in Carolyn Shoemaker's name...

That's... not a meteor...
"So..."

...what are we actually looking for?

I've been talking to some other campers, and for a few days now, there have been sightings of a "glowing entity" near the river that VANISHED before anyone could catch up to it!!

All CLASSIC alien signs! So, I'm headed to the river to check it out!
About that...

Look, Emily, we've all seen lots of weird, supernatural stuff at this camp, right?
Yeah! Roller skating bigfoots and everything!

And I get the feeling we haven't seen nearly everything that's out here...

So what makes you think THIS thing--whatever it is--is extraterrestrial and not just...well, roller skating bigfoots?

I don't expect you all to understand, it's okay! But I've been hunting for aliens for most of my life now, and I know a thing or two!

This is FOR SURE aliens!

Sooo...

What's this REALLY about?
Don't know what you mean.

Hes. Are you SERIOUSLY here to help Emily hunt for aliens? Why did you pull me along?

C'mon.

Fine! Fine... you're right...

COUGH COUGH
wanted to ask your advice.
HEM!

What was that?

UGH, FINE, I wanted to ask your advice.
Seriously?

What can I do for y--
It's...relationship advice.

W-what? Why me?!

Isn't it obvious?

What...what are you--
Hey, hey, don't stall out on me... I didn't think this would be like, A REVELATION to you.

Jo! Did you know Molly and I were CAMP COUPLE?
Sure.

WHAT?!
You're just going to have to face facts... you two are really cute!

How long have you known?!
Wouldn't you rather know...

...who HES is crushing on?!

Whaaaat? Hes, you LIKE somebody?!
How is this the FIRST we're finding out about this?
Sure, let's everyone talk about this...

It's not a big deal! But if you MUST KNOW...
We MUST!
Eh, I don't care.
Shush!

It's...uh...

DIANE!
Knock it off!

Don't JOSTLE me, you don't want me accidentally dropping a star onto Jupiter or something.
Jen? I can see the star too, it's... getting bigger?
Alright. No one panic. We're going to be calm about this.

Stop whatever it is you're doing, Diane!
Woah, woah, I wasn't actually DOING anything! I was just messing with April!
HOW DARE!
Then stop THAT!

I'm going to talk to Rosie. Everyone keep cal--

eeeKRONCHEEEWWW-WOOP!

ATTENTION LUMBERJANES! SOME SCOUTS HAVE NOTICED A RATHER LARGE SHOOTING STAR SEEMINGLY HURTLING RIGHT TOWARDS US.

NOW, IT'S PROBABLY NOTHING, BUT WE **ARE** GOING TO--
--Well, "take cover" sounds alarming--
--WE'RE GONNA SCOOT ON QUICK-LIKE OVER TOWARDS THE TREES!

AHHH!
TAKE COVER!
TAKE COVER!
PANIC! AT THE ASTRO
WE'RE GONNA GET SQUISHED!

AAAHHHHHH

WE'RE TOO LATE!!

SNAP.

WE'RE OUT!

GRR! DIANE, YOU--

POOF!

BOOF

FOOM
POOF!

Girls?! G--Scouts? Are we all okay?
KOFF
KOFF

BEHOLD, MORTALS!

HA HA HA HA HA!
IT IS I!

THE GODDESS FREYA!!

WHAT?!
9

will co

The u
It help
appeara
dress f
Further
Lumbe
to have
part in
Thiskw
Hardc
have
them

THE UNIFORM

should be worn at camp
events when Lumberjanes
n may also be worn at other
ions. It should be worn as a
the uniform dress with
rect shoes, and stocking or

out grows her uniform or
ther Lumberjane.
ia she has
her
her

FRIENDS!

TAKE COVER!

The
yellow, short sl
emb
the w
choose
slacks,
made o
out-of-do
green bere
the colla
Shoes ma
heels, rou ... ings or
socks shou ... the shoes or wi
the uniform. Ne... bracelets, or other jewelry do
belong with a Lumberjane uniform.

HOW TO WEAR THE UNIFORM

To look well in a uniform demands first of
uniform be kept in good condition—clean
pressed. See that the skirt is the right length for your own height and build, that the belt is adjusted to your waist, that your shoes and stockings are in keeping with the uniform, that you watch your posture and carry yourself with dignity and grace. If the beret is removed indoors, be sure that your hair is neat and kept in place with an inconspicuous clip or ribbon. When you wear a Lumberjane uniform you are identified as a member of this organization and you should be doubly careful to conduct yourself in a way that will show everyone that courtesy and thoughtfulness are part of being a Lumberjane. People are likely to judge a whole nation by the selfishness of a few individuals, to criticize a whole family because of the misconduct of one member, and to feel unkindly toward an organization because of the

The unifor
helps to cre
in a group.
active life th
another bond
future, and pr
in order to b
Lumberjane pr
Penniquiqul Thi ... Lady
Types, but m ... will wish to have one. They
can either bu ... or make it themselves from
materials available at the trading post.

GET TO WORK, GIRLS!

LUMBERJANES FIELD MANUAL

CHAPTER SIXTY-SIX

Back in the Lumberjanes' Mess Hall, the GODDESS FREYA delights the 'Janes with tales of her adventures!
...On and on, the battle raged! First hours passed, then DAYS! Still I fought, separated though I was from my vanguard of Valkyries!
The Jötunn, the Frost Giants, now had me surrounded on all sides...but one!
Yes! My back was to the sea-- I could taste the salt and hear the icy waves CRASHING hundreds of fathoms below the rocky cliff--
But height means NOTHING to FREYA, and her FALCON'S CLOAK!
I FLEW from the cliff's edge! And THERE! On the horizon! Braving the crushing waves of ice!

SKÍÐBLAÐNIR! HUZZAH!
SkiP...blot... near?

Skíðblaðnir! My brother Freyr's magic hanky that unfolds into a MIGHTY SHIP!
Ooooooh...wicked!
I DOVE towards the ship, where I met with Freyr and Thor! Together, we SHATTERED the Frost Giants...

...and drove them from Vanaheimr!
Hey, Diane, can YOU fly?

Wh--I, ye-- if I FEEL LIKE IT, 'KENZIE!

HAHAHA!

POP!

GULP

HUZZAH!
ANOTHER ROUND OF JUICE FOR ALL!!
HUZZAH!

Bonk!
Clap
Clap
You, uh, drank ALL the juice we had...

Cool story. You fought tall cold people. Wow...

...Nothin' like that around here, though, right, April? Besides...
FREYA

...we're pretty much all set on goddesses, so--
TRULY? Tell me, which of my kin has graced you all!

Frigg? Iðunn? Loki, in one of his more feminine moods?
FREYA

It's ME!
I'm a goddess!

So, Freya, tell us what brings ANOTHER goddess to the Lumberjanes camp!

LO! I was on a simple journey! A mere jaunt across the Rainbow Bridge of Asgard, when what did I see atop a grassy hilltop?
A GATHERING OF ENCHANTING MAIDENS!
I, FREYA, HAD TO STOP AND MARVEL AT SUCH A FLOCK!
YAY!

And how fortuitous that I did! Never before have I encountered so many fiery young maids, outside the very VALKYRIES OF VALHALLA!
FREYA

BY FRIGG'S FORESIGHT! Truly, I am reinvigorated to see such SPIRIT still dwells in the mortal realm!
Pray, O Happy Janes of Lumber, what can Freya do for such a luminous troop of daughter-kin to mark this merry meeting?!

Huh?
Do? What do you mean?
A ***BOON***, SWEET MAIDEN MOLLY!

HUH?
AH HA HA HA! It has truly been too long since Freya has visited!

A **FAVOR,** dear 'Janes! It will be my honor to share with you once again the majesty of A GODDESS!
I'm not buyin' it!
FREYA

DIANE!
What's your GAME, huh? What sort of goddess just throws favors around willy-nilly?
C'mon, Diane! Be cool!
Yeah, let us get a super awesome goddess wish!

Freya plays no game! What sort of deity would I be if I did not share with you some WONDERS OF THE GODS, for brightening my day?!
ACTUALLY. They already know all about that wonder and junk. 'Cause I'M here!
OF COURSE!

...Which goddess were you again?
I'M--
"Seriously?!"

DIANE!!!

See? This is why I didn't want to say anything.
Sorry, Hes, it's just...

...Diane is who you like? Really? She's...uh... sort of grump--
But she's so **mean**?

Yeah, well. You don't know her like I do, Mal...
Then tell us.

I mean...
She's cool, and really funny, but in, like, a subtle, sarcastic way...like, you have to be paying attention?
And she doesn't pick on anyone who can't dish it back, not since she got back from Olympus.
And she's really been *trying*, you know? I can see her making an effort, 'cause she cares about us, and she loves camp just as much as us, an--

WHAT?!
Oh, my gooooosh!

You LOVE Diane.

Hey, now, c'mon. Let's not throw around the "L" word...
I don't think I've ever heard you talk so much at once!
And I've NEVER seen you so flustered!
OH, MY GOSH, YOU LIKE HER **SO MUCH!**

I regret this entire day.

Okay, enough mushy stuff! Back on task!
PAT PAT

We've got EXTRATERRESTRIALS to track down! Right, Jo? Ripley?
YEAH!

For the last few nights, scouts have noticed a glowing, floating figure in the woods...

...when approached... it vanished! Leaving behind...

...a crop circle!

ALIENS!!
What did it look like?!
Emily. In WHAT crops?
gulp
TRUE SAD

Okay, not CROP circles...but there was for sure a weird pattern in the grass!

HA!
...So, I can't draw super great, but...you get the idea.

It's something!

Keep your eye out for crop circles!
Hes...

Seriously, though... Have you TOLD Diane all that stuff about her you like? She'd probably love it.
Maybe, but...

She's a LITERAL GODDESS, y'know? She probably hears that stuff all the time...
Hmm...and she doesn't need an even BIGGER ego...

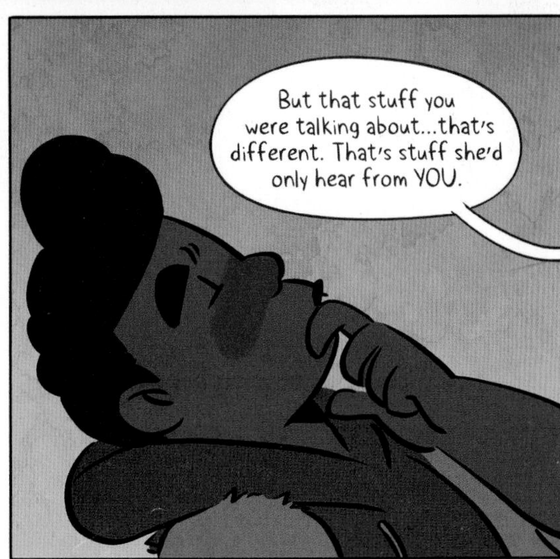
But that stuff you were talking about...that's different. That's stuff she'd only hear from YOU.

I can't hear what they're TALKING about!

Diane's probably getting in trouble for trying to fight a goddess. What's WITH her today?!

Well, we're missing a **certain** Zodiac who has a calming effect on her...

ABOUT ***that...*** I haven't seen Mal, Jo, Ripley, OR Hes and the other Zodiacs since we got to the outlook, and--
It's fine.

Wren told me.
April was busy fighting with Diane, I think...

...Wren, Emily, and Hes are looking for aliens, or whatever, and your missing cabinmates went with 'em.

They'll catch up.
Whoa, whoa. Jo went on an E.T. adventure *without* me?
Sorry, April. I thought you two knew.

But--
It's fine.

Hes is with them. They'll be fine.

Hey! You in trouble for almost starting an epic GOD FIGHT? 'Cause I kinda wanted to see that...
FWOMP!
NO. Rosie just asked me to be...

...polite.
AH! THERE you are!

Freya here is going to take a look around our camp!

She'll need a guide, though! And I thought--
GAAASP!

What do you want to see first? There's LOTS!
YEAH!
May I ask questions about your pantheon? What can you tell me about your rainbow bridge?
What do you BENCH?

AH HAH HA! Such SPIRIT!

YOINK!
Haha, yeah, we know ALL the best spots!

What's your angle, Diane?
Just being polite.

Who better to show a goddess around than another goddess?
INDEED! Lead the way, My Guides!

Guess what? "The Valkyries" is the name of my ice hockey team!
GLORIOUS! Tell Freya of this "Iced Hookey"!

Sure! C'mon, I'll show you the sports equipment shed!
Boring! Let me show you the outhouse that DINOSAURS come out of!

You want to show her a toilet?
THAT DINOSAURS COME OUT OF!
ONLY SOMETIMES!
I LIKE this goddess!
Do you think she'd sign my "It's a Myth-tery" badge?

CRUNCH.
10
CLICK
BAM!
POP!

HaHaHa!
HUZZAH!

Ha Ha Ha!
9

HOP!

OOO! How high in the air could you throw me? I'm, like, extremely dense, matter-wise!
HAH HAH! I KNOW NOT!

LET US FIND OUT!

Wheee!

Hey.

Don't you want to hang out with everyone's new best friend?
Actually...

...I need a little break from her. She's...a lot. It's like her caps lock is always on, or something...

HA! YES, EXACTLY! SHE--

ahem. Yeah.

Are you just saying that to cheer me up?
Heh.
I don't know about you all...

......but I am POOPED.

I need a break...

Z Z Z
She sure likes Marigold...
HUP!

SHRIIIIIINK

DASH!!!

Uh.
Is she...

She's...

SHE IS!
SHE'S CATNAPPING!
BUD, SHE'S TOTALLY STEALING YOUR CAT!
AH!

Ha!

HA! I KNEW it! I KNEW IT!
What did I say, huh? She--

Oh, right.

Let's get her!

will co…

The u… It he… appearan… dress f… Further… Lumbe… to have… part in… Thiskw… Hard… have… thems…

…HE UNIFORM

…hould be worn at camp …vents when Lumberjanes …n may also be worn at other …ions. It should be worn as a … the uniform dress with …rect shoes, and stocking or

…out grows her uniform or … …ther Lumberjane. …a she has … her … her

The… yellow, … emb… the w… choos… slacks, … made o… out-of-d… green ber… the colla… Shoes ma… heels, rou… …ngs or socks shou… …h the shoes or wi… the uniform. Ne… …es, bracelets, or other jewelry do … belong with a Lumberjane uniform.

HOW TO WEAR THE UNIFORM

To look well in a uniform demands first of … uniform be kept in good condition—clean … pressed. See that the skirt is the right length for your own height and build, that the belt is adjusted to your waist, that your shoes and stockings are in keeping with the uniform, that you watch your posture and carry yourself with dignity and grace. If the beret is removed indoors, be sure that your hair is neat and kept in place with an inconspicuous clip or ribbon. When you wear a Lumberjane uniform you are identified as a member of this organization and you should be doubly careful to conduct yourself in a way that will show everyone that courtesy and thoughtfulness are part of being a Lumberjane. People are likely to judge a whole nation by the selfishness of a few individuals, to criticize a whole family because of the misconduct of one member, and to feel unkindly toward an organization because of the

The unifor… helps to cre… in a group. … active life th… another bond… future, and pr… in order to b… Lumberjane pr… Penniquiqul Thi… …core Lady Types, but m… …es will wish to have one. They can either bu… …, or make it themselves from materials available at the trading post.

LUMBERJANES FIELD MANUAL

CHAPTER SIXTY-SEVEN

Deep in the woods, the Lumberjanes are hot on the trail of extraterrestrial life...
They go this way!

Is it an alien? Are they alien tracks?
TRU

We don't know what their feet would look like--
Absolutely!

Uhhhh...

C'mon, Jo, why aren't you willing to trust me on this stuff?!
We have to think about this scientifically, Emily! You're assuming too much!

We already have so much proof about what aliens look like, though!
I don't know about "proof"--
TRUE SAD

I'M GONNA FIND THE THING!

CAREFUL, RIPLEY! PEOPLE ON THEIR OWN HAVE A HIGHER CHANCE OF BEING ABDUCTED!!
THERE'S LITERALLY NO SCIENTIFIC DATA BACKING THAT UP!

If we get abducted, I'm blaming you, Hes!
Hey, you're the one who followed US, Wren!
TRUE SAD

Okay, then it'll be your fault if MAL gets abducted, and HER GIRLFRIEND will take revenge on you!
Hahaha! You're bright red!
Wh--Hey, M-Molly is--
ARGH!
TRUE SAD

"I wonder what the others are up to. Probably nothing as exciting as alien hunting!"
I'm only saying...

...I was right all along! I KNEW Freya was up to no good!
Those Norse gods are ALWAYS trouble.
We HEARD you, Diane!

Sooo...? All I'm looking for is a little acknowledgement, alright, April?
9
9

No! Not the time for gloating!
Barney's really upset about the catnapping!

Wh-why would someone STEAL Marigold?!

Marigold's AWESOME, that's why!

BAW
You're not helping!

ARGH! I just can't WIN with you people!

SKIIII'D!!!

huff
huff
huff
What is it? Why are we stopping?

I...don't know
which way Freya went...

What if we
can't catch her?!
sniff.

What?
ahem
I don't know. Are you
going to bite my head off if
I SUGGEST something?
NOT IF IT'S HELPFUL!

Oh!

Diane is ARTEMIS!
Greek goddess of
the moon, the wilds,
childbirth--
Don't forget
protector of young
girls, Molly.

--and goddess of THE HUNT!

I'LL track down that thieving phony!

TWEEEE!

This'll be fun! I haven't been hunting all summer!
POOF!

THERE they aaaare!

THERE are my good boys!

Ahem! **Wubby! Doughnut!**
We're hunting a thief, who stole a cat...

...that smells like THIS mortal.

Snuff! Snuff!
Hahaha!
Snuff!

They've got the scent!

What?

Wubby and Doughnut?
I named them when I was, like, TWO! Okay?!
I think they're nice names!

I just didn't know you were so SWEET! I guess if dogs like you, you can't be THAT bad!
HEY! Rude!
"Ripley!"

RIP! WAIT UP!

Phew. You haven't been abducted.
The tracks stopped.

WHAT?!

ARGH!

I was SO CLOSE!
I WAS **SURE** OF IT!

...Probably beamed back to their ship already...
TRUE SAD

...Probably wasn't even aliens...
TRUE

Emily. Why is this so important to you?
Yeah, what's up?
sigh... It's STUPID.
No one here is going to think that. Promise.

We're all weirdos.

My parents run an alien-themed cafe...
"...I LOVE it."
EXIT
EARTH OR BUST!
RED PLANET DINER

"But...I get teased about it..."
I WANT TO BELIEVE

I had this crazy idea when I saw all the impossible stuff in these woods... if I could **prove** there were aliens...

...I don't know... then people wouldn't make fun of me and my parents...
Emily...

...I wanna to go to your restaurant SO! **BAD!**

Yeah. Sounds cool.
Do you get free food?
Sometimes. But I have to use my own quarters for the pinball machine.
THERE'S A PINBALL MACHINE?!

YOU'RE THE LUCKIEST KID IN THE WOO-O-ORLD!

Something made those tracks...

...and it's not even dark yet! How are we supposed to find any glowing entities in the daytime?

SNIF I think I want to keep looking. For a little while, anyway.
I never want to STOP!

Yeah! Let's find an alien!
Until it gets dark. Then we go back to camp!
Deal...

"...and thanks."
Yup. This is a magic feather, all right.

Looks like she tried to fly off...

...but she had to land again--
Are we close?

AAOOOW!

Jeez, Diane!
Isn't that a little extreme?!

thwip!

ARGH!

Whoa! Nice SHOT!
Yeah!
Eh, I was aiming for her leg...

WHY ARE YOU CHASING ME?!

Wh--?

YOU ARE RUNNING!

BECAUSE I'M BEING CHASED!

No, DUH! 'Cause you CATNAPPED Barney's cat!

What? I did no such thing!

Uhhhhh...

YA KINDA DID!

Oh, no.
No, no. You do not understand, dear Mackenzie.

THIS is FREYA'S cat! VANISHED from Freya's home!

Freya is simply recovering her and taking her to her rightful home.
You're wrong! Marigold has been with me since she was...

...born? Came into existence?

So, this cat just, what? Poofed into existence?
You've never heard of magic cats before? Psh.

OR...

...was she
TELEPORTED
here...

"...from SOMEWHERE ELSE?"
We were close before... those tracks led from one crop circle to another...

...and now we're at the river, where all the sightings happened, right?
Right.

And we're in a bush, because...?
Because we don't want to frighten it away.

It's smart! Aliens are famously shy!

gasp!

Ripley!
I see it!

GASP!

I can't look. Is it another yeti with a disco ball? A werewolf with a candelabra? Mothman carrying a flashlight?

Look!

WHOA!
HAHAHA!
AH!
EMILY! WHAT NOW?
I--AHH!

AHHH!

click.

It's STARING at us.
Uh. Now what?
I don't know! I didn't plan this far ahead.
Uhhhh...

"...Does anyone...have any questions for it?"
What if...what it that's TRUE?

I mean, it COULD be, right? We don't really know where the kittens came from...
Noooope! Nuh-uh. That's dumb. This is all dumb.
THAT is my #1 favorite nap buddy...
...and 100% THEIR cat.
Now GIVE. HER. BACK.

Uh, Diane? Freya?
Let's all just--

Wait up a second, Molly...

...this is getting
PRETTY RAD...

mmmr

Hey!

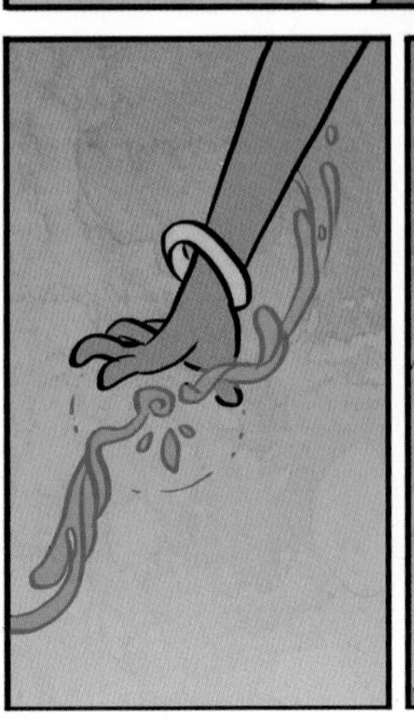

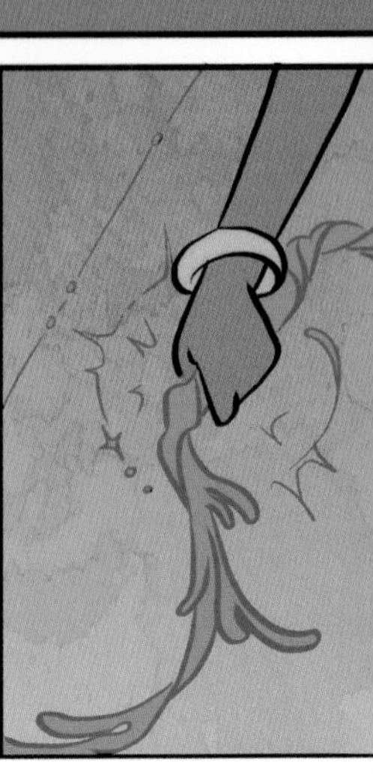

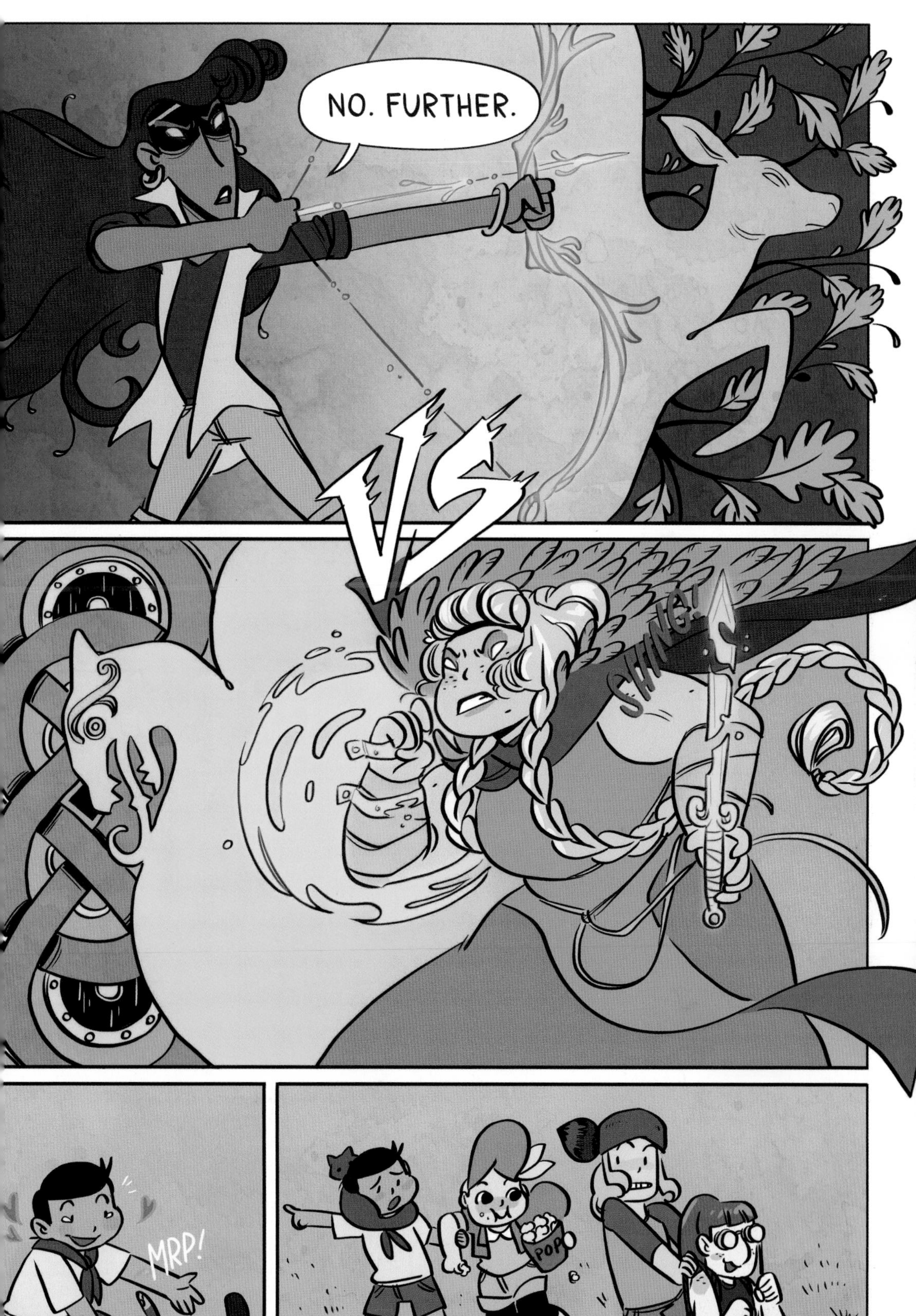
NO. FURTHER.
VS
SHING!

MRP!

POP

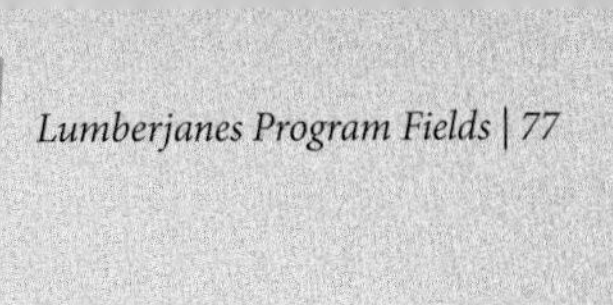

will comm

The ur
It helps
appeara
dress f
Further
Lumbe
to have
part in
Thiskv
Hardc
have
them

THE UNIFORM

should be worn at camp
events when Lumberjanes
n may also be worn at other
ions. It should be worn as a
the uniform dress with
rrect shoes, and stocking or

out grows her uniform or
to another Lumberjane.
insignia she has
her
her

OH, GODS!

GANGWAY!

The
yellow, short sle
emb
the w
choos
slacks,
made o
out-of-do
green bere
the collar a
Shoes may b
heels, round t ... ings or
socks should c ... with the shoes or wit
the uniform. Ne... ces, bracelets, or other jewelry do
belong with a Lumberjane uniform.

HOW TO WEAR THE UNIFORM

To look well in a uniform demands first of
uniform be kept in good condition—clean
pressed. See that the skirt is the right length for your own height and build, that the belt is adjusted to your waist, that your shoes and stockings are in keeping with the uniform, that you watch your posture and carry yourself with dignity and grace. If the beret is removed indoors, be sure that your hair is neat and kept in place with an inconspicuous clip or ribbon. When you wear a Lumberjane uniform you are identified as a member of this organization and you should be doubly careful to conduct yourself in a way that will show everyone that courtesy and thoughtfulness are part of being a Lumberjane. People are likely to judge a whole nation by the selfishness of a few individuals, to criticize a whole family because of the misconduct of one member, and to feel unkindly toward an organization because of the

The unifor
helps to cre
in a group.
active life th
another bond
future, and pr
in order to b
Lumberjane pr
Penniquiqul Thi ... ore Lady
Types, but most l ... janes will wish to have one. They
can either buy the uniform, or make it themselves from
materials available at the trading post.

NOT HELPING, DIANE!

LUMBERJANES FIELD MANUAL

CHAPTER SIXTY-EIGHT

In the woods outside of camp, the legendary goddesses Diane and Freya battle for the right to bring Marigold the kitten home...
CLANG
FWIP!
P-TING!
huff huff
YOU HAD ENOUGH YET?!
huff huff huff
NAY, FOE! FREYA HUNGERS FOR MORE!

LEST YON JANE OF LUMBER SUBMIT THEIR KITTY TO FREYA!
WE TOLD YOU ALREADY, THAT AIN'T YOUR CAT!
AND STOP TALKING SO WEIRD! IT'S DISTRACTING!
Okay...who knows how we STOP two goddesses from battling each other?
What? Why is everyone looking at me?
You're our general expert on MYTHS, Molly!
Yeesh, April, I don't--

THOSE TWO MYTHS OUT THERE ARE GOING TO LEVEL THE FOREST!

Well, the stories aren't helpful! Most disputes from mythology end with someone turning someone else into, like, a musical instrument, or creating an island, or inventing some NEW NATURAL DISASTER!

So EPIC!
YES! IT IS **LITERALLY** EPIC, MACKENZIE!

mrrowp
!
Oh! Sorry, Marigold!
SQUEEEEZE!

Sorry, everyone...

Don't YOU apologize 'cause a giant lady is trying to steal YOUR cat, Barney!
SNIF

POP!

HEY, YOU!

YEAH, YOU! YOU'RE MAKING MY SWEETEST CINNAMON ROLL OF A FRIEND FEEL BAD FOR NO REASON!
!

HURGH!
HA-HAH!

RAH!
WAAH!
KICK
FLIP

huff
huff

Okay.
You're pretty good...

...lemme just...

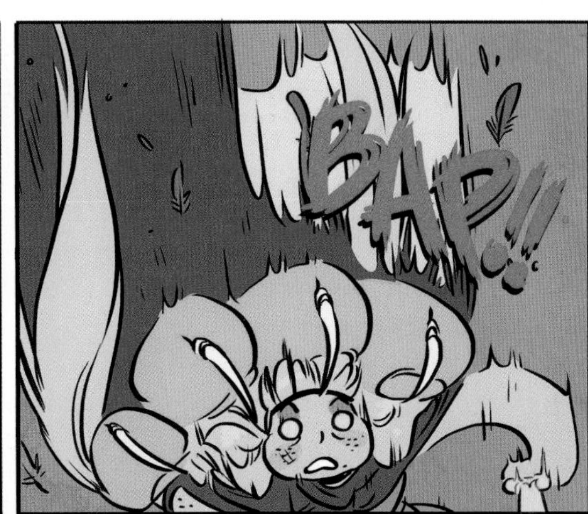
BAP!!

MRP!

Or...that works, too.

I WON! YES! I--

purr
purr
purr
Good girl, Marigold!
You stay right there!
You need a time-out!

Now, FINISH HER, Marigold! There's a good kitty!
DIANE, NO!
I yield.

I yield.

sigh.
I had so wished for this to be the missing cat I search for...but...

...alas, I have been deceiving you all...

...I am NOT the goddess Freya.
Called it.

I am the goddess IRPA!
Irpa...I don't think I've heard of you.

NO ONE HAS!
I...borrowed Freya's feathered cloak and chariot to visit the mortals and I... lost one of Freya's cats!

If I return without him, Freya will tie me to a rock and let a giant serpent drip venom on my face 'til the end of days!!
Sweet Sarah Bernhardt, that's dramatic!
Supes harsh.

THAT'S THE KIND OF STUFF GODS DO TO EACH OTHER!!

Sigh.

There, there. We Lumberjanes--sigh--help people and are compassionate and stuff...
FLUMP.

...we can help you look for this cat...

"...what does it look like, or whatever."
Is it just me...

...or does that alien look like a giant, glowing cat?

Did a scouting lad lose their cat?
I don't remember anyone having a giant, glowing cat, Wren...

purr purr purr
Awww! It LIKES me!

Do you think that's an alien cat?

...It's probably a magic cat, Emily.
Yup, it's totally a magic cat. DANGIT.

Y'know, you might have better luck with more open spaces...corn fields and spots like that...
Definitely.
You think?
Thanks, Jo.
I bet that picture you took will still look really cool!
Hey, you're right! Maybe my parents can hang it up in the restaurant!
Yeah!
Uh! Guys? It's doin' something!
Ripley! Let go of it!
But--

AAAAH!
BOOSH!

Huh. So that's what caused the crop circles.
RIPLEY!

We're never going to catch up to them! It's already getting dark out!

BONK!

HAIL AND WELL MET!
BONK X2!!
...Hi?
MAL!
MOLLY?!
Where have you BEEN?!
Long story.
Who is that?
Long story.

Where's--
SHE'S FALLING!
WAAH!
POOF!
POOF!
OOF!
Thanks, Di.
Of course, Hes.
HEEEERE, KITTY KITTY!
Here, kitty kitty!
Shuck Shuck Shuck

Prrwp? !
COME GET DIN DIN!

PURR PURR PURR
HAH HAH! SUCCESS!

So that's...
A Norse goddess.
And the cat?
TRUE SAD
9

Pulls a magic chariot.
POOR LAD WAS TRYING TO FLY HOME ALONE! HE CANNOT WITHOUT HIS BROTHER!
Now...

Allow Irpa to ferry you fair 'Janes back to your camp!
WOO-HOO!
HUZZAH!

XENA

Wow. A catnapping and everything...

Good thing you had Diane with you, huh? Goddess of the hunt and everything, right?

THANK YOU!!!

Hes, you're the only one who gets me.

THERE you all are!
It's okay, Jen!

We were with Irp--Freya the whole time!
Mostly.

Well, I'm afraid we won't be able to observe the meteor shower from the overlook...

...there's a large, goddess-shaped crater there now!
FRET NOT, HONORABLE JEN! LET ALL KNOW TO GET ATOP THEIR DOMICILES!

HA HA!
EVERYONE GET ON YOUR ROOF!
Should I be concerned about this...?
Astrophysically speaking... this will probably be fine!
Probably.
Hey, Diane...

It was pretty cool of you to help Barney get Marigold back... you're a good friend to them...
Yeah. You too, April.
I suppose you're not the worst...either.
Thanks. I guess what I'm trying to say is...
Let's never hang out.
I am so happy to hear you say that! I couldn't agree more!
SNAP
LESS HOSTILE!!!
WOW! They Don't Want To Kill Each Other!!!!
PAP.
Better Than Nothing
They are so ODD.
Yeah.
TRUE SAD
C'mon! I don't want to miss the show!

Oooooh!
Aaaaah!
SMOS
LUNA
ECL
Wow, you were hunting for space-aliens that whole time?
I was surprised about it, too.
ROANOKE
Hes needed my help, though, so I was like, "All right, we can hunt for aliens for a little bit, but I have to get back to camp. M-my...my girlfriend is waiting for me."

Wh--did y--I...
I can't believe my girlfriend is an alien hunter!
hahaha!
UGH.
That was exhausting. Today has been exhausting.
FLOP!
Hey, Diane. Thanks for looking out for the other Zodiacs while I was gone.
Sure.
And y'know... I DO get you...

...I've noticed that you're trying to be nicer. And I wanted to tell you...just, that I've noticed that.
H♡D
ALSO, YOU'RE PRETTY, AND I LIKE YOU A LOT.
Whoa.
...Yeah.
I, uh...
...I like you, too. But I don't have any interest in kissing, or junk like that...
With anybody?
Nope. Never have.
Oh.
I didn't know that was a thing...

Wait! You like me back, though?! Like, romantic-style?
Yeah...more than I've ever liked anyone...
Okay. Cool. Heh.
Yeah.
So, um...
...what about...?
That would be nice.

HUZZAAAH!
NEXT: FORESTRY IS THE BEST POLICY!

will co…

The u… It h… appeara… dress f… Further… Lumbe… to have… part in… Thiskv… Hardc… have … them…

…E UNIFORM

…hould be worn at camp …events when Lumberjanes …n may also be worn at other …ions. It should be worn as a … the uniform dress with …rrect shoes, and stocking or …

…out grows her uniform or …ther Lumberjane. …a she has … her … her

The… yellow, short sl… emb… the w… choos… slacks, … made o… out-of-d… green bere… the colla… Shoes ma… heels, rou… …ngs or socks shou… …with the shoes or wi… the uniform. Ne…es, bracelets, or other jewelry do… belong with a Lumberjane uniform.

HOW TO WEAR THE UNIFORM

To look well in a uniform demands first of … uniform be kept in good condition—clean … pressed. See that the skirt is the right length for your own height and build, that the belt is adjusted to your waist, that your shoes and stockings are in keeping with the uniform, that you watch your posture and carry yourself with dignity and grace. If the beret is removed indoors, be sure that your hair is neat and kept in place with an inconspicuous clip or ribbon. When you wear a Lumberjane uniform you are identified as a member of this organization and you should be doubly careful to conduct yourself in a way that will show everyone that courtesy and thoughtfulness are part of being a Lumberjane. People are likely to judge a whole nation by the selfishness of a few individuals, to criticize a whole family because of the misconduct of one member, and to feel unkindly toward an organization because of the

The unifor… helps to cre… in a group. … active life th… another bond… future, and pr… in order to b… Lumberjane pr… Penniquiqul Thi… …ore Lady Types, but m… …es will wish to have one. They can either bu… …, or make it themselves from materials available at the trading post.

The Lumberjane uniform

...m, or make it
...able at the trading post.

...tivities. ... is a
...right red neckerchief is ... neath
... be tied in a simple friendship knot.
... lack or brown and should have flat
... a straight inner line. Stockings or
... nd in color with the shoes or with
... aces, bracelets, or other jewelry do not
... erjane uniform.

...WEAR THE UNIFORM

...orm demands first of all that the ...ood condition—clean and well ... is the right length for your own ... belt is adjusted to your waist, ... kings are in keeping with the ... our posture and carry yourself ... dignity and grace. If the beret is removed indoors, ... sure that your hair is neat and kept in place with an inconspicuous clip or ribbon. When you wear a Lumberjane uniform you are identified as a member of this organization and you should be doubly careful to conduct yourself in a way that will show everyone that courtesy and thoughtfulness are part of being a Lumberjane. People are likely to judge a whole nation by the selfishness of a few individuals, to criticize a whole family because of the misconduct of one member, and to feel unkindly toward an organization because of the

The ... helps ... in a g... active ... another ... future ... in or... Lumberjane ... Penniquiqul Thistle Cr... Types, but most Lumberjanes wi... can either buy the uniform, or make it them... from materials available at the trading post.

COVER GALLERY

Lumberjanes "Out-of-Doors" Program Field

IT'S A MYTH-TERY

"Tell me lore, tell me lore."

Stories predate the printing press, libraries, and even writing itself. Myths and legends, fables and folklore are passed down from generation to generation across the years, as well as continents wide, and oceans deep. We create them and share them, and in turn, they create us as well, by becoming the building blocks of our cultures. They teach us our values and what we believe, and they hold us together, across diaspora and against the ticking of the clock. We remember our ancestors, the world they lived in, and the things they believed through the stories they left behind.

There are myths that hundreds and thousands of people are familiar with— the ones that are shared across an entire culture or religion, that tell us how our world was created, the origins of life, or about the gods, goddesses, spirits, and demons who favored and helped, or disapproved and hindered the humans of legend. These tales are often written down in books nowadays, but they date back to the oral tradition, to stories told around a campfire, or sung in the form of a ballad. Some are sacred. Others might be silly, but they continue to be told— to echo throughout time, like a river wearing through a canyon. Try looking them up at your local library, and explore the stories of Hunahpu and Xbalanque, Thor and Loki, Oshun and Shango, or Osiris and Isis.

Consider if you have any examples of legends within your own family. It might surprise you to find that you do—stories that have been told again and again down the years, so often that even baby cousins who were far too tiny to have remembered an event themselves will have some awareness of it. The story has taken on a power of its own now, beyond just telling you all about your grandmother or great-aunt. Your family has chosen to remember this tale, to hold it dear, to repeat it so often that everyone knows the details, the beats, the morals. This story has become one of hundreds of tent posts that make your family what it is. It tells you who you are, as a group, and what it is that you care about, both on a grand and minor scale.

Issue Sixty-Five
KAT LEYH
88

Issue Sixty-Five Preorder
SAS MILLEDGE

Issue Sixty-Six
KAT LEYH

Issue Sixty-Six Preorder
SAS MILLEDGE

Issue Sixty-Seven
KAT LEYH
SAD

Issue Sixty-Seven Preorder
SAS MILLEDGE

Issue Sixty-Eight
KAT LEYH